MAX E. JAMES

CRASH COURSE

J. RYAN HERSEY

Illustrated by Gustavo Mazali

D1004636

TABLE OF CONTENTS

To my parents – whose adventure with their grandchildren sparked the idea for this book.

FREE DOWNLOAD

Will Max's one and only birthday wish come true?

Join my Kids' Club to get your free copy of the second book in the Max E. James children's series. Type the link below into your browser to get started.

http://eepurl.com/cfcfkj

Chapter 1

Rocket Racer

BEEP.

Beep. Boop.

I yanked my covers back and rubbed my eyes.

Beep. Boop. Beep.

What is that? I thought, cracking an eye. Flashes of color crept under the door and shadows danced across the wall.

Beep.

Beep. Boop.

I bolted out of bed. "Cody!" I said.

I wrapped my favorite blanket, Fuzzy, around me, and ran toward the sound. I burst into the living room and found Cody playing Rocket Racer all by himself. Well, almost. Curled up next to him was my puppy, Birthday Miracle.

Beep. Beep.

"No wonder you always win," I said. "You're practicing without me."

Cody paused to look up.

"No," he said, "I win because I'm a better racer."

Birthday Miracle yawned as I patted her head. "Cheater," I said softly.

"I've only played two games," Cody said.

"You know it's not fair to practice without me," I said. "You promised."

He shook his head.

"And," I said, "you know we're not allowed to play Y-Cube this early. If Mommy found out, you'd be in big trouble."

"I never heard that rule," he said, turning back to the game.

"Yes, you did. I was there! Mommy!" I called out.

Cody dropped the controller and cupped his hands over my mouth.

"Shhhhh! Please don't wake them up," he said. "Just let me just finish this game. You know I'll lose rocket points if I quit now."

He picked the controller up and continued playing.

"It's not fair," I said, reaching for the controller. "You'd better turn it off."

"Stop," he said, mashing buttons furiously. "You'll make me wreck and I'm in second place."

"Turn it off or I'm telling," I said.

Beep. Boop.

"Just two more turns," he said, still staring at the screen.

I clenched my teeth and lunged for the controller. He snatched it away, but his car lost control and crashed.

He glared at me and pointed at the screen. "Look what you did!"

I turned to see all the other racers zooming past the smoldering wreckage of Cody's car.

I grabbed the controller. "Good," I said. "Now it's my turn."

"Oh no you don't," he said. "I call do-over."

I turned away, covering the controller. "You've already had your turn," I said.

I hit the reset button and the car rolled to the starting line. Cody looked at me, then back at the TV.

Three. Two. One.

The green light flashed, and I screamed out of the starting gate.

Yes! I thought. *It's finally my turn to play.*

Click.

The screen went blank.

"What?!" I said. "What happened?"

I spun around to face Cody. He was leaning against the wall, swinging the TV cord in a circle.

"I guess it's nobody's turn now," he said. "Good luck playing without any power."

I frowned.

"You know, Max," he said. "I think I do remember that rule. No Y-Cube before 8:00 a.m., right?"

"No way!" I said. "You can't pick and choose when you follow the rules."

He shrugged his shoulders. "Rules are rules," he said, letting the cord come to a rest. "Unless of course, you want to settle this fair and square?"

I put the controller down. "I'm listening."

"How about a friendly race?" he said. He plugged the TV back in and grabbed another controller.

"Best out of three laps?" he said. "Winner gets to play again."

"Deal," I said, squeezing his hand as hard as I could.

We peeled off the starting line and zoomed around the track. I pulled in front of him at turn two. He was on my tail as we spilled onto the straightaway. I glanced at him after the first lap. He just smiled.

I cruised around the second lap just ahead of him, my body jerking with every turn. As we rounded the corner to start the final lap I thought,

This is way too easy. Something's up.

"Winner takes all," I said.

"Watch this, Max," Cody said.

His fingers blurred as he pressed a flurry of

buttons and his car shot out in front. He pressed faster and a black oil slick splashed onto the track behind him. I hit the slick and my car spun off the track.

The checkered flag dropped, and Cody won.

"Level five oil slick?!" I said. "How'd you get that?"

He smiled. "I unlocked the code while you were asleep."

"That's not racing!" I screamed. "I never had a chance and you know it!"

Cody rolled his eyes and turned to the screen. "Better luck next time," he said. "Now, where was I?"

My face felt hot and my heart thumped in my chest.

"Do-over!" I screamed. "And no oil slicks this time."

"Don't be a sore loser," he said, reaching for my controller.

At that exact moment, a shadow stretched across the floor. We both froze. Mommy walked through the door. Cody glanced at her as I cupped my hands over my mouth.

She walked past us and unplugged the game. The screen went dark and she walked back into her bedroom with our beloved Y-Cube, never saying a word.

"Great," Cody said. "Now nobody gets to race."

"Doesn't matter," I said. "You cheated."

Cody shook his head. "Whatever."

"Bet I could beat you in a real race," I said.

He laughed. "Yeah, right."

"Watch me," I said and walked into the garage. Cody followed close behind.

"Okay, Speedy-Britches," he said. "Let's see how fast you really are."

We opened the door and slipped into the cool, grey morning. I stopped at the foot of the driveway and waited for Birthday Miracle.

"What's the matter, Max?" Cody asked. "Having second thoughts?"

Birthday Miracle darted through my legs into the yard.

"Nope," I said. "Just curious to see how it's going to look."

"What?" he asked.

"Your face when you eat my dust," I said as I took off past him.

Chapter 2

Mom, Can I Borrow the Car Keys?

"SO, WHERE'S IT going to be?" I asked.

"Well," he said, "the driveway is pretty straight."

"I guess so," I said. "Seems fair."

Crunch. Crunch.

I shuffled my feet, stomping down the gravel as I walked my lane.

Crunch.

"What in the world are you doing?" Cody asked.

"I need it flat," I said. "I can't take any chances."

Cody crossed his arms and ground the toe of his shoe into the gravel. "Okay," he said. "The first one to the mailbox wins. Ready?"

"You're on," I said.

"On your mark. Get set."

"Wait!" I said. "Wait a second."

"What now?" Cody said.

I bent over and touched my toes. "I almost forgot to stretch," I said. I swung my arms in huge circles and jumped up and down.

Cody sighed.

"What about now?" he asked. "All warmed up?"

"Almost," I said, jogging in place.

I looked down the driveway and gulped a huge breath.

Cody tapped his foot. "Quit stalling. Are we going to do this or what?"

"All right," I said. I crouched into my stance and pressed my hands into the gravel. "Ready when you are, but no cheating."

"Don't worry, Max," he said. "I don't have to cheat to beat you."

I bit my lip and stared down the driveway. "We'll just see about that," I said softly.

"Take your mark," he said. "We'll go on three."

I closed my eyes and swallowed against the knot in my throat.

"One ... two ..."

My heart pounded in my chest.

"Three!"

I dug my toes into the gravel and was off like a shot.

Crunch. Crunch. Crunch.

I tore down the driveway, pumping my arms as fast as I could.

Crunch. Crunch. Crunch.

I couldn't see Cody, but I didn't dare turn to look.

Wait, I thought. *Am I winning?*

Crunch. Crunch. Crunch.

I was halfway to the mailbox, but still couldn't see Cody. My legs ached and my lungs were on fire. I couldn't keep this pace up much longer.

Crunch. Crunch. Crunch.

I couldn't take it. I had to know where Cody was, so I looked back over my shoulder. He was behind me, only by a step, but I was actually beating my big brother!

I turned back just in time to see Birthday Miracle charge onto the driveway.

"Arrgh!" I screamed. "Puppy!"

She tucked her tail and darted across my path.

Crunch. Crunch. Boing.

I leapt over her and soared through the air, but when I landed the gravel slid.

Wham!

I crashed to the ground and tumbled forward.

Cody sped past me and began to walk. With a grin, he strolled to the mailbox and tapped it.

"I win," he said.

My eyes burned, and I bit my lip.

"No fair," I said, wiping my sleeve across my face. "The dog tripped me!"

Cody helped me up and brushed me off. "Are you all right?" he asked. "That was a gnarly fall."

I rubbed the gravel off my stinging knees.

"I guess so," I said. "I would have beat you if I hadn't tripped."

Cody smiled and rubbed my head. "I don't know about that, but you're definitely getting faster."

"I was winning!" I shouted. "You know I was."

"Who says I wasn't just making it a little more interesting?"

"Yeah, right," I said, kicking the ground.

Thunder rumbled softly in the distance of the hazy sky.

"Come on," Cody said. "Let's go in."

We walked in and Mommy was already setting the table for breakfast.

"What were you guys doing out there?" she asked. "Is it raining?"

"No, just cloudy," I said. "We raced for real since you took away Rocket Racer."

Cody smiled. "Yeah, and I won."

"Only because Birthday Miracle tripped me," I said.

He shook his head. "Anyway," he said, "what are we going to do now?"

"Beats me," I said. "We can't even play the Y-Cube."

Daddy walked in. "I'll never understand kids

today. It's like you'd rather play video games instead of experiencing things for real."

"What do you mean?" I asked. "We can't race real cars!"

Cody flicked my ear. "I'd totally beat you if we could," he said.

I squinted at him.

"It doesn't matter anyway," I said. "We're like thirty-seven years away from driving."

Mommy giggled.

"You don't have to be that old to drive," she said.

I jumped up on the chair and towered over her. I looked down and in my deepest voice I said, "Mom, can I borrow the car?"

Everyone laughed as I stretched out my arm and pointed to my open hand. "I need the keys, please."

Daddy walked over and dropped the keys into my hand. "Sure, Max," he said.

My face lit up. This trick had never actually worked before.

"Only one condition," Daddy said. "You have to be that tall without the chair."

"That's a dirty trick," I said, handing back the keys.

Daddy smiled. "You have a few years to go, but you'll be driving before you know it."

"Hmmm," Mommy said. "There might be a way."

"What are you talking about, Mommy?" I said.

"Yeah," Cody said. "A way for what?"

"For you to drive in less than thirty-seven years," she said.

We were paying full attention now. The room was silent.

"I don't know," Daddy said. He pulled back the curtain. "It looks pretty grim out there. Those places close when it rains."

"Or," she said, "if the weather holds out, we'll have the tracks all to ourselves."

"Hmmm," he said. "No lines either?"

"Nope," she said.

"Wait a second," I said. "Rain, tracks, driving, lines?"

Mommy knelt and smiled. "How would you two like to race for real?"

CHAPTER 3

What If I'm Not "THIS" Tall?

TWO HUMONGOUS CHECKERED flags marked the entrance. We sprinted across the parking lot and stopped just past the flags. Thunder rumbled softly in the distance.

"Come on," I called back to Mommy and Daddy. "Hurry up!"

We gazed toward the track closest to the entrance. Old tires lined the asphalt that snaked through the park.

Mommy and Daddy caught up to us while we watched. "See, guys?" she said. "It's basically empty."

We ran further into the park searching for the

ticket counter. That's when I noticed the bazillion bowls of goldfish.

Goldfish? I wondered. *What in the world are fish doing at a race track?*

I wandered past the fish tables and found myself smack in the middle of a tiny carnival.

"What is all of this?" I asked.

Cody appeared beside me.

"I don't know," he said as he ran past. "But it's so cool!"

There were goldfish bowls to throw ping-pong balls at, balloons to throw darts at, ring toss, and all sorts of other awesome games.

Cody grabbed my shoulder and spun me around. "Look at that," he said.

He pointed to a huge kiddie pool that had a platform on one side and what looked like huge, crumpled plastic bags piled on top.

"Do you know what that is?" Cody asked, clapping his hands together.

I shook my head.

"It's Bubble Bouncer!" he said. "You get inside the bubble and they blow it up. It's like a hamster wheel for kids—in water!"

"Wow," I said.

I just stared. We had never actually seen Bubble Bouncer except in TV commercials.

That's when I felt a hand on my shoulder.

"Okay, guys," Mommy said. "The ticket counter is this way."

"Oooh! Mommy," I said, "can we do the Bubble Bouncer? Please?"

Her face got all scrunchy. "I don't think so," she said. "Do you two have any idea how many germs are in those things? And we're here for the go-karts, not carnival games."

I looked at Cody. He shook his head, agreeing there was no way we were going to win this one.

"Look," Mommy said. "Your father is already at the ticket booth. Let's go."

I shuffled my feet and looked back over my shoulder. "I guess I'll see you in my dreams, Bubble Bouncer."

Cody laughed. "Come on, Max. This is going to be great."

Mommy shivered. "More like Booger Bouncer," she said softly. "Those things give me the creeps."

We zoomed over to the ticket counter.

"Four tickets, please," I said. "We want to ride all the go-karts."

The worker appeared at the window and smiled. "I'm sorry, but four tickets will only get you four rides," she said.

I frowned. "We need way more than that," I said. "How about a million?"

Daddy coughed. "What other options do you have?"

"Wristbands," she said. "They'll let you ride as much as you want for three whole hours."

"Sounds good," Daddy said.

"You sure picked a good day to come," the

worker said. "There aren't many people racing today. The weather must have scared them off."

She strapped on our wristbands. "Okay, just one more thing."

I was admiring my bright pink wristband when she appeared with a cardboard cutout. It was of a kid holding up a sign that read: "You Must Be This Tall to Ride This Ride."

My heart skipped a beat and sunk deep in my chest.

"What is that?" I asked, looking at Cody. "What if... what if I'm not this tall?"

Cody giggled. "Don't worry, Max," he said. "I'm sure you can ride with Mommy."

The worker set the sign next to me. I slinked up beside it and stretched out as tall as I could. I stood on my tippy toes and pretended to be a giraffe.

"Nice try," she said, "but I think you have some growing to do."

"Aw, rats," I said, kicking the ground. "I knew this was too good to be true."

"Don't worry," she said. "You can still ride by yourself. Just not the super-fast go-karts."

She moved on to check Cody's height. I shook my head and turned away. I already knew he was tall enough.

Daddy walked over and rubbed my head. "It's for your own safety, Max," he said.

"He's right," the worker said. "There's only one kid I know who's been allowed to ride the super-fast go-karts without meeting the height requirement—and that's the track owner's kid who basically grew up here!"

I looked up at the worker. "But I'm a good driver," I said. "I promise. I play Rocket Racer every day."

The worker chuckled. "I'm sure you are, but racing real go-karts is way different than playing video games."

Wispy, grey clouds rolled in the distance as we arrived at the first track. It was called "The Drifter." No one else was waiting so we strolled right into the pit where the cars sat sputtering.

I went for the go-kart in the front. Cody got into the one beside me. Mommy and Daddy settled in behind us. The worker came by and snugged down our seat belts. He paused when he got to me.

"Hmm," he said.

My tippy toes were barely touching the gas and brake pedals. I slid further down in the seat and stretched to press the gas.

Vroom. Vroom. Vroom.

The engine roared and the kart vibrated.

He winked, buckled my seat belt, and made his way off the track.

I glanced over at Cody.

Vroom. Vroom. Vroom.

We gawked at the other racers on the track as they zoomed past the starting line.

The worker pointed to lights in front of us: red, yellow, and green. The red light was on.

"Okay, racers," the worker said. "When the light turns green, that means go!"

I clenched the steering wheel and watched the red light. Engine exhaust hung thick in the air as I took in a deep breath. The light clicked from red to yellow.

Vroom. Vroom. Vroom!

I swallowed hard and everything went silent as I stared at the yellow light. Any second now I'd be out on the track, racing for real.

The light turned green and as I stomped the gas the silence was shattered.

Screech!

CHAPTER 4

I Guess We Missed This One

THE TIRES SPUN as plumes of gray smoke twirled in the air. The kart slid back and forth trying to grip the track.

"Yee-haw!" I screamed. "We're burning rubber now."

The tires snagged the asphalt and my head snapped back as I shot onto the track.

When I reached the first turn, I stomped the gas pedal and wrenched the wheel left. I felt the back of the go-kart start sliding. The next thing I saw was Mommy, Daddy, and Cody swerving to miss me. I was facing the wrong direction!

"Later, Max," Cody called on his way by.

I turned the wheel as far as it would go and

pressed the gas. I had only turned around halfway when the go-kart slammed to a stop.

Wham!

I blasted into the bumpers lining the track. I tried the gas again, but the tires just squealed and smoked. I was stuck.

"What?!" I said. "These cars don't go backward?"

Now what? I thought. *I'm strapped to a car that*

can't even back up. I flailed my arms and yelled for the worker.

"Help!" I said. "I'm stuck!"

I searched the track for help as the other go-karts buzzed around again.

Zoom! Zoom! Zoom!

The roar of their engines quieted, and my car magically began moving.

"Hey!" I said. "It does go backwards." I pressed the gas and the go-kart lurched forward into the rail again.

"Hold on a second, little buddy," a voice called from behind me. "Stop pressing the gas. We have to get you turned before they come back around."

The worker tugged at the seat and moved the go-kart so I could make the turn.

"That should do it," he said, looking toward the track. "Here they come. You'd better get going."

"I will," I said, cranking on the wheel and pounding the gas.

Vroom!

I sped forward, leaving a trail of black streaks. This time I let off the gas before the turn so the back wheels didn't slide.

Chirp. Chirp.

The go-kart skipped across the track as I

rocketed out of the turn. I could see the other racers up ahead.

Here I come, I thought. *I'm going to get you now.*

I sped down the track and coasted through the next turn. The rear of the go-kart didn't spin out this time. I slipped around the corner and *bam!* The kart snapped into a straight line.

"Woo-hoo," I cheered. "I'm getting the hang of this."

I just need to turn better, I thought. *Like in Rocket Racer. The tighter the turn, the faster you go.*

I grabbed the steering wheel and just as I started to turn—

Whoosh!

A purple streak shot past me. The wind swept across me and rocked my go-kart.

I sped up to try and get a closer look at who had passed me. The driver was too small to be Mommy or Daddy, and too fast to be Cody.

"Who was that?" I said softly.

I tried to keep pace with the purple car as it squeaked between Mommy and Daddy, but it was no use. The driver was just too fast. I managed to catch up with Mommy and Daddy and pulled alongside them at the next corner.

"Hi Mommy," I said. "Hi Daddy."

They smiled and waved. "Glad to see you're going the right way," Daddy said. "You have to watch those turns."

Mommy clutched her steering wheel and stared straight ahead. "Not too fast now, Max."

"Don't worry," I said as I slingshot past her. "There's no such thing!"

The purple go-kart was right behind Cody as they approached the next turn. But when Cody pulled into the turn, the purple racer swerved and cut him off.

I giggled and stomped on the pedal.

Chirp... chirp.

Their wheels brushed together, and the purple car slid out of the turn in the lead. Falling to second place distracted Cody enough to let me catch up.

"I've got you now!" I said. He turned into the curve, so I jerked the wheel hard and sped to the inside.

"Rookie move!" he yelled as he jammed his kart back into the turn.

Screech!

His go-kart scraped against my bumper. "Hey!" I screamed. "No bumping!"

We filed onto the straightaway and I held the wheel perfectly straight to inch alongside him.

No way, I thought. *Am I going to pass him?*

"Watch this, Cody!" I shouted.

Blah-bloom.

My go-kart rumbled and shuddered.

Blah-blam.

It slowed to a crawl as Cody pulled away.

Brumble. Brumble.

The engine grew quiet and I coasted down the track. I stepped on the gas.

Click. Click.

"Aw, nuts!" I said, smacking the steering wheel.

Cody waved over his shoulder as he pulled out of sight.

"Just when I was going to beat Cody for the first time ever," I said.

Vroom.

Mommy flew past me.

Wind blasted across my body every time a car passed. I sat still in the middle of the track.

"This isn't racing," I said.

The checkered flag fluttered off in the distance. I crossed my arms.

Humph.

The race was over, and all the other go-karts had pulled off the track while I sat, strapped in my bum go-kart.

Blam.

The go-kart jolted forward and started rolling. I turned around and was eye-to-eye with the same track worker from before.

"This just isn't your lucky day, kid," the worker

said. "First you're stuck in the turn and now you're out of gas."

"Gas?" I said.

"Yup," he said. "We usually fill them up in the morning. I guess we missed one."

"Aw, man," I said. "I was beating my brother too."

He smiled. "Sorry about that, little buddy. You'll have to get him next time."

He pushed me back to the pit and unbuckled me. I thanked him and slipped off to join my family.

"What happened to you?" Mommy asked.

I frowned. "I ran out of gas," I said, "and the go-kart just stopped."

"Too bad," Cody said. "You almost caught up."

We walked off the track.

"Besides not winning," Daddy said, "how was driving a real go-kart?"

I smiled. "Awesome," I said. "It was way better than any video game could ever be!"

"Yeah," Cody said. "Let's trade the Y-Cube for a go-kart."

Daddy shook his head.

"Did anyone else see that purple go-kart?" I asked.

"Only as it passed me," Cody said.

"That driver was super-good," I said.

"And lightning-fast," Cody said. "I thought I was doing okay until that kart flew by."

I looked back at the track and saw the purple go-kart, but the racer was gone.

"Forget about it. Let's go to the next track."

"You guys go ahead," Mommy said. "I think I'm going to sit this one out."

"Me too," Daddy said. "We'll watch you from the sideline."

Cody looked at me. "Race you!" he said. And without letting me answer, he took off.

CHAPTER 5

Yellow Means Go Faster!

THE WIND PRESSED firmly against my chest as we scrambled to the next track. I stopped at the entrance of the Grand Prix track; there were two lines.

"Which one?" I asked.

"Beats me," Cody said. "Just pick one."

He darted left, and I followed. There were only a few other people in line. I hung onto the fence and stared across the twisting track. Its coils reminded me of a mad snake.

"Come on, Max," Cody said, nudging me forward.

"Good. Good. Okay. Next," someone said as the line shuffled forward.

Cody was next.

"Good," the track worker said and waved him on.

I walked forward, paused, then continued onto the track. I spun around when I felt a hand on my shoulder. I realized I hadn't heard an "okay."

"Hold on just a second, buddy," he said, pointing at two huge rulers attached to the fence beside him. "Sorry, but I need to check your height. Stand over here, please."

I towered over the first ruler.

"Yes," I said softly.

"No problem there," he said. "Now how about this one?"

He pointed to the other ruler and my heart sunk. I watched Cody as he hopped into a yellow go-kart. I took a deep breath and stepped forward. The backs of my legs burned as I inched up on my tippy-toes.

He smiled warmly, but I knew he was just being nice.

"Sorry, little buddy," he said. "You're just a tad too short."

"But I'm taller than the first one," I said. "So, I can ride, right?"

"Yes and no," he said. "One ruler is for fast

go-karts and the second is for the super-fast ones. Only one type can race at a time."

I was confused. "But there's only one track," I said.

He nodded. "We color coded the cars so we can tell them apart," he said. "The green go-karts on the left are fast and the yellow ones on the right are super-fast."

"That doesn't make sense," I said.

"What doesn't make sense?" the track worker asked.

"Green go-karts should go faster than the yellow ones because green means go."

The worker chuckled. "Yes," he said, "but yellow means go faster."

I frowned.

"You can ride the green one," he said, "but that means that everyone has to race green."

He blew his whistle. "Green go-karts," he said. "If you're racing, get a green go-kart."

My cheeks felt hot as I walked onto the track and picked a go-kart. I heard a few racers groan, so I sank down behind the steering wheel. Apparently, they needed to go super-fast, not just fast. I stared at the yellow go-karts across the track and buckled up.

"One day," I said softly.

The worker gave a thumbs-up. "Okay," he said. "Is everybody ready?"

All the racers screamed and hollered.

"Just remember to watch out for the puddle at turn six," he said.

The light went from red to yellow, then to green.

I stomped the gas and we were off in a puff of smoke.

Slow? I thought. *No way! This is fast!*

I cruised past the track worker and pulled behind Cody onto the first straightaway.

Cody took the first turn and I was right on his tail. He cut the corner close and I took it wide. I brushed against the outside rail and jerked the wheel back toward him.

"You're not getting away from me that easily," I said. When I hit the next straightaway, I ground the pedal into the floor.

Cody funneled into the next hairpin turn and almost lost control. The back of his go-kart slid sideways and let out a puff of smoke.

Varoom.

That's when a car zoomed past on the outside. The racer looked familiar.

I hit the turn at full speed and the wheels chirped

around the corner. The go-kart slid back and forth, clinging from turn to turn as I tried to catch Cody.

Up ahead something sparkled on the track.

What is that? I thought, squinting to see ahead. *That must be turn six.*

Everyone swerved to miss it. The huge puddle stretched across most of the track. The racers ahead were barely squeaking by.

I jerked my go-kart out of the way just in time to miss it. "Whew," I said as my tires cut through the edge of the puddle, spraying a light mist into the air. "That was close."

I cruised out of the turn and saw the other racers up ahead. The racer who'd passed me was already passing Cody.

"Wait a second," I said. "I know who that is! It's the mystery racer who beat us on the other track. Racer-X!"

Cody tried to take the lead as the laps ticked away, but it was no use. By the time the worker raised the white flag signaling the final lap, I was right behind Cody.

I have to do it now, I thought. *It's all or nothing.*

Cody was only a few feet ahead of me. I shot around a turn after him and cut sharp to the inside. We were bumper to bumper through the turn. The tires squealed as I pulled out in front for the very first time.

"Woo-hoo!" I screamed. I slammed on the gas and sped down the straightaway. I couldn't believe I was winning.

"Woo-hoo!"

Gak.

Awk.

Something flew right into my mouth! It slammed into my throat and hit that little dangly thing in the back.

Awk.

I let go of the wheel and batted my tongue, but whatever it was, was too far back to reach. That's when it wiggled.

"Ahhhhh! It's—"

Awk.

"—alive!"

Awk.

"Phaa-tooey!"

I spat out a slobbery glob of wings and legs as I rubbed my eyes. When I finally opened them, I was staring straight at turn six.

I grabbed the wheel, but it was too late. My front tires were already slicing through the water. The tires slid and the go-kart spun around in a circle. I blasted right through the turn, skipped over the barrier, and skidded into the grass.

Varoom.

"Bye, Max!" Cody screamed as he passed. "Better luck next time."

I slapped the steering wheel as water dripped from my face. I stomped on the gas, but it was no use. The wheels just spun and spun.

I pawed at my tongue to try and get any last bug pieces out.

Awk.

Great, I thought. *Not only did I lose the race, but what if that bug pooped in my mouth?!*

I scraped at my tongue with my shirt sleeve. "Yuck!" I said.

That's when I heard footsteps. A track worker appeared out of nowhere. "That puddle will get you every time."

I nodded.

He pushed me back onto the track. "Okay," he said. "Hurry back to the pit. They're starting another race."

When I pulled up to the pit, the other racers were already pulling onto the track.

"Grab one quick if you want to be in this race," the track worker said, taking off for the starting line.

I jumped into the closest go-kart and pounded the gas. The tires screamed and my head slammed back in the seat as I fired out of the pit.

Vroom!

"Wow," I said. "This go-kart is way better than the last one." I shot down the straightaway and blasted through the first turn. I couldn't believe how fast I was catching up to the other racers.

That's when I noticed what color my go-kart was.

Chapter 6

Pit-Pat! Pit-Pat!

IT WAS YELLOW! I was in a yellow go-kart! I searched the track ahead and saw a sea of green. *This is awesome!* I thought.

Sce-rerh-rerh-rerh-rerh.

Then I hit the straightaway and gassed it. I squealed around the second turn and hugged the outside of the track.

"Wow," I said, "when they say super-fast, they mean it."

I caught up to the other racers and saw that Cody and Racer-X were battling for position just ahead of me. Racer-X swerved back and forth, blocking Cody from passing.

I was coming up fast as they squeaked by the puddle at turn six.

Va-room!

"There you are," I said. I stomped on the pedal and blew past them on the outside.

"Woo-hoo!" I said. "Yellow means go faster."

I waved as I passed. Up ahead I saw someone on the track. He was waving his arms and pointing to me.

"Stop!" he called as I drove closer. I stomped on the brakes and screeched to a halt. He leapt out of the way just as I pulled up.

Vroom. Vroom.

All the cars I had just passed zoomed by.

"Hey buddy," he said. "You're in the wrong color go-kart!"

"I know," I said. "The yellow one is way better than the green one! Did you see how fast I caught them?

He chuckled. "I suppose I did."

"Can't I stay in this one?" I asked. "Just for a few more laps?"

"I wish it was that easy," he said. "But I don't make the rules."

"But I was doing so good," I said.

"You were," he said, "but it's not fair and you're not tall enough to drive that one."

I pulled into the pit and switched go-karts, then pulled back to the starting line.

"Hold on," the track worker said. "They're coming around again."

Cody and Racer-X were neck and neck with the other racers close behind.

Vroom.

Vroom. Vroom.

They screamed past like a swarm of angry bees.

"Okay," the track worker said. "Now you can go."

I stomped on the gas and sped onto the track in last place.

Wow, I thought. *This one's not nearly as fast as the yellow one.*

I would have to race my best to catch up to the pack. I hit the first turn and passed a straggling car. I slipped past another one on the straightaway. After a few laps, only one car was left between me and Cody.

The very next turn I pulled into third place. Cody and Racer-X were side by side and I was hot on their trail.

I got you now, I thought.

We barreled onto the straightaway and I gained on them. I knew the turn ahead was my chance to make the pass.

Pit-pat.

Something stung my cheek.

"Ouch!" I said. "What was that?"

Pit-pat.

Pit-pat.

Crack! Boom!

Thunder crashed and lightning sparked across the sky.

I looked up at the dark clouds just as the sky broke open. In seconds my clothes were drenched, and I could hardly see the track.

The rain poured down in sheets and splashed onto the asphalt.

Out of the corner of my eye, I saw a flutter of orange. It was the track worker flagging everyone into the pit.

"Get off!" he yelled. "The track's closed." He pointed and swung the flag.

We funneled into the pit to park the go-karts.

I pulled in behind Cody. "I almost had them," I said softly.

Everyone hopped out and took off for the covered awnings near the carnival games.

My water-logged feet sent ripples through the puddles as we tromped through them. We stopped at the edge of the awning to catch our breath.

"Did you see me, Cody?" I asked. "Did you see me?"

"No, Max," he said. "I could barely see anything."

"I accidentally drove a yellow go-kart!" I smiled. "It was super-fast!"

"So that's how you passed me so easily," he said.

I nodded.

"I was so busy trying to beat that mystery racer," Cody said, "that I didn't notice the color."

"You mean Racer-X," I said. "That dude is fast. Where'd he go, anyway?"

"Beats me," Cody said. "I lost him in the rain. I like the name though."

We scanned the soaked crowd, but Racer-X was gone. I spotted Daddy waving to us from the other side of the awning.

"Over here, guys," he said. "I found a dry spot."

We ran over to meet him.

"Did you see us racing?" I asked.

He nodded. "Looked like you guys were having a blast. Too bad the weather didn't hold up."

"I know," I said. "What are we going to do now?"

"I don't know," Daddy said. "Racing might be done for the day though."

"Where's Mommy?" Cody asked.

"She went to grab an umbrella," he said. "She'll be back in a minute."

"The carnival games are dry," Cody said.

"I guess we could check them out," Daddy said.

I smiled and whispered in Cody's ear, "Now's our chance."

He grinned.

"Awesome, Daddy," he said. "Bubble Bouncer looks fun!"

"Yeah," I said. "I've never been in one of those before."

Before Daddy could answer, we sprinted to the platforms beside the pool where the deflated plastic bubbles were resting.

Daddy caught up to us. "You want to do this?" he asked. "Are you sure?"

"Yes!" we screamed.

"It's like a giant hamster wheel in water," I said.

"It will be great," Cody said.

"Well," Daddy said. "We do have a few minutes to spare. And it looks like the rain is already letting up."

We peeked out from under the awning and sure enough, as quickly as it had started, the rain was almost over. It even looked like the sun was trying to peek through the clouds.

"Hold on a second, boys," Daddy said. He had a quick chat with a track worker then came back to us.

"What'd he say?" I asked. "Can we still race?"

"They're going to check the tracks now," he said. "It all depends on how wet they are."

"So," I said, "can we try the bubbles?"

"You might as well," the track worker said. He walked up behind us and put his hand on Daddy's

45

shoulder. "I can have them in the water in less than a minute."

Daddy looked down and smiled. "Okay, boys."

"Great!" Cody and I said together.

"Hop onto the platform and I'll do the rest," said the worker.

We jumped up and stood in the center of the clear lumps of plastic.

"Okay," the worker said, lifting the plastic up around us. "Step into that zipper part while I hook up the blower."

We stepped in and he turned the blower on. The bubbles inflated around us like huge balloons.

Once the bubbles were almost filled, the worker sealed the plastic flap. Air whirled around my head as the bubble stretched into a plump ball. He disconnected the blower, and all was quiet.

I knocked on the wall of the bubble. "What now?" I asked.

He pointed to the pool of water below the platform. "Just start running!"

I looked at Cody. The worker had finished sealing him in too.

I gave him a thumbs-up and jolted toward the pool. The ball rolled forward and flopped off the platform.

CHAPTER 7

Bubble Bouncer

I BOBBED IN the water and took my first step inside the bubble. The spongy plastic rolled under me and I fell flat on my back.

"Whoa," I said, rocking back and forth while I tried to brace myself.

I looked over just as Cody rolled off the platform and plunged into the pool.

Small waves from Cody's splash rippled against my bubble. It was super squishy and I couldn't control it. I tried walking slowly, but that didn't work. And when I ran faster, it would move faster, and I'd fall flat on my face.

"Humph," I let out a breath and teetered back and forth in the water. Cody was next to me struggling to stand. He smiled through the shimmering plastic.

"This is a lot harder than it looks," I said. I smacked the wall and fell forward. "How do you work this thing anyway?"

Cody gave me a thumbs-up and then lost his footing. His face disappeared and all I saw were socks and skinny legs.

I wobbled to my knees and crouched for a few steps.

Nice, I thought. *Now I just have to stay up.*

The bubble turned slowly as I walked, pretending I was on a tight rope.

I looked over at Cody. "I think I'm getting the hang of this," I said.

He nodded his head, but never took his eyes off his feet. He took baby steps and turned his bubble toward me and grinned.

"Raminator power!" he screamed and bobbed toward me, sloshing through the water.

Splash!

Cody smacked into my bubble, knocking me over.

"Hey!" I said. "No fair."

Cody's laugh echoed through the plastic.

"You should have seen your face, Max," he said. "Totally priceless."

I scampered to my feet and slowly rolled away from him. "That should be good," I said softly.

I leapt across the bubble and sprinted toward him. The water churned as I tried to keep up with the spinning ball.

Wham!

"Take that, Cody," I said, knocking him off his feet.

I fell forward and rolled up the side of the bubble, then back down the other.

Cody was lying on his back staring at me.

"Now you know what it feels like," I said.

Cody rose to his knees and braced his arms across the bubble.

"It's so hard to balance," he said.

"I know," I said.

"Watch this," Cody said. He wobbled to his feet, tucked his head, and flipped forward. He landed flat on his back and bounced back up to his knees.

"Did you see that?" he asked. "It doesn't even hurt."

"That flip was awesome!" I said.

"Pretty sweet, right?" he said, rocking back and forth. "You try."

"I don't think I can."

"You'll never know until you try," he said.

I looked down through the clear plastic where bits of leaves and grass danced below me. I tucked my head and tumbled forward into a clumsy roll. I stared at the roof of the bubble and swayed back and forth.

"That wasn't a flip," he said. "I don't know what that was."

"It's hard to balance in here."

"Watch," Cody said. "Like this."

I watched his bubble bounce up and down after he landed on his back again.

"Like that, Max. Now you try."

"Okay," I said, pulling myself up. I tottered in the center of the bubble. "One ... two ... three!"

I leapt into the air and tucked my head. The world outside whirled in a blur as my feet smacked down.

Rip!

Splash!

I landed right on the seam holding the bubble closed and slid right through.

"Ahhhh!" I screamed as cool water gushed in. "I popped my bubble!"

My feet hit the bottom of the pool and I stumbled in waist-deep water as the flimsy plastic collapsed around me.

"It's closing in on me," I said. "Somebody help!"

I looked over and saw Cody right beside me. He was rolling with laughter, rocking up and down. "Max," he managed between laughs, "what in the world are you doing?"

I grabbed my flabby bubble and slogged over to the platform.

"Get me out of this thing," I said. "I can't breathe."

I thrashed about, trying to get a leg onto the platform, but the water-logged bubble dragged me backward.

The worker grabbed the plastic and jerked me up onto the platform just as I was slipping back into the pool. Water poured from my clothes as the worker opened the seam and the bubble fell around me.

"Are you all right?" the worker asked. "What in the world are you guys doing out there? Nobody's ever popped one of these before."

"Just having a little fun," I said.

I hopped down and saw Mommy standing beside Daddy near the entrance. She did not look happy.

I walked over to them, leaving a trail of soggy footprints. "What?" I said. "It opened."

"Ugh," she said. Her lip curled upward, and her eyebrows slanted down. "Gross. I can't believe you guys got in those."

She scrunched her nose and looked at Daddy.

"What?" he said. "It looked like fun."

She opened her purse and grabbed some hand sanitizer—the jumbo bottle.

"You come here," she said. "Do you know how

many germy little kids have slobbered and snorted all over those bubbles?"

I shook my head.

"Probably more than I can count," she said. "They've coughed, drooled, spit...."

I looked up at her. "And?" I said.

"And?" she said, leaning in closer. "And some of them probably even passed gas in there."

I looked at Daddy, who was trying not to laugh, then I bent over, laughing so hard I couldn't breathe.

Cody pulled me to my feet. "You know," he said, "they did smell a little funky."

"Yeah," I said, "Mine was a little sticky."

"Ewwwww," she said. "Give me your hands."

She squirted sanitizer into my hands and scrubbed furiously. Then she lathered my arms.

"Ouch, Mommy," I said. "It burns."

She just kept rubbing and squirted a huge glob onto my forehead.

She snapped a look at Daddy. "And you," she said. "I was only gone for two minutes. And you shove them into a life-size used tissue!"

I decided it was better to just keep quiet. She smeared more hand sanitizer across my face and down my neck. I closed my eyes and held my breath in burning silence until she was finished. I blinked my eyes and another figure came into focus.

"You too, Cody," Mommy said. "Come over here so I can clean you up."

I shook my head in agreement.

"Um. Okay," he said. He walked over slowly, and I was free.

"Wait! Mom-my!" he said. "What are you doing? That's hand sanitizer, not body sanitizer."

She paused. "Hmmm," she said, reading the label. "You're right. So, I guess the only way for you to get clean would be to go home and take a shower, right?"

I stopped laughing and squinted at Cody.

He grabbed the bottle and splashed it onto his neck.

"You missed a spot," he said.

She smiled. "What's the big deal, anyway? The tracks are closed."

"Still?" I said. "What did the workers say, Daddy?"

"Nothing yet," he said. "But by the looks of it, we're done for the day."

Just then an announcement came over the loud-speakers. "Attention. May I have your attention, please," the announcer said. "Due to rainy conditions, all tracks but one are closed."

"Awww," the crowd moaned.

The announcer continued. "The Grand Prix track is the only track open. Rain vouchers are available at the office on your way out."

I watched helplessly as the crowd of disappointed racers shuffled toward the exit.

"Can we stay?" I pleaded. "We didn't even get to finish our race earlier."

"Yeah," Cody said. "Look how long the line is." He pointed at the mob near the ticket booth.

"Look," I said, "it's right there. We're going to walk right by it on our way out."

Mommy looked at Daddy and he hunched his shoulders. That's when I noticed a kid running through the corner of my eye. I tapped Cody on the shoulder. "Look," I whispered. "Over there."

We stood and watched as Racer-X ran to the Grand Prix track and jumped into the lead go-kart.

CHAPTER 8

What? Racer Who?

I BATTED MY eyes and smiled, waiting for Mommy's answer. Cody slid up beside me and joined in.

"Well," she said, "I don't see the harm since it's on our way out. But this is the last one."

"Yay!" I leapt in the air and almost knocked Cody over. "Thanks, Mommy!" I said.

"You're the best," Cody said.

She pointed to the track. "Better hurry, it looks like you have some competition."

"Pssssttt. Cody," I said, elbowing him. "That's Racer-X."

Cody smiled. We sprinted over and hopped into two go-karts.

"Looks like it's only you three," the track worker called from the starting line. "So, we'll race three laps, but watch out for turn six."

Racer-X and Cody are going to need the luck

this time, I thought. *This is my last chance for some real racing.*

Vroom. Vroom.

I revved the engine and stared at the lights.

Red.

Yellow.

I dug my nails into the steering wheel.

Green.

Screeeeeech!

I stomped the pedal and tore out of the pit. Racer-X sped around the first corner and into the lead.

We zoomed through the first lap in single file. There was only one time Cody even got close to Racer-X, and then he had to slam on his brakes, swerving to miss the monster puddle at turn six.

One lap down, I thought. *Only two left.*

We bolted past the pits and zoomed into the first turn bumper to bumper. My tires chirped as I clenched the wheel, trying not to slide across the seat.

I was slowly gaining on Cody. At the next turn I took the inside lane and pulled up beside him.

He shot me a glance. "No way, Max!" He slammed on the gas and cut back in front.

"Cody!" I screamed. "Racer-X is pulling away. This is our only chance to win!"

We cut through the next turn and I pulled up to Cody again. "Together!" I screamed. "We have to work together."

I saw the puddle ahead and dropped back to miss it.

We cruised through turn six and the engines roared as we spilled onto the straightaway. We passed the start and the track worker waved the white flag. It was the last lap!

We screamed through the turns in single file. Our bumpers rubbed back and forth as we fought for position and motored again toward turn six.

This is it, I thought. *Now or never*. Racer-X cut wide outside at the next turn and squealed around it. Bits of tire and gravel peppered my face, but I held my position.

Cody took advantage and swerved inside to pull up beside Racer-X as we headed for turn six. I was right behind them, and my bumper brushed against the back of Racer-X's go-kart. I could feel my heart pounding as the engines screamed. I was ready to make my move.

That's when it happened. Cody didn't let off his gas. He was right beside Racer-X heading for the puddle. He slammed through it at full speed and a wave of water exploded over Cody and Racer-X.

The force of the water and shock of the splash slowed them down. That was the only chance I needed. I turned the wheel, stepped on the gas, and closed my eyes. Water sprinkled across my face as I felt the go-kart pulling out of the turn.

I wiped the gritty water from my face and opened my eyes. All I saw in front of me was track.

"Yes!" I screamed. "This is it."

I flamed down the track, pressing the pedal as hard as I could.

"There it is," I said. "The finish line!"

I couldn't look back. The checkered flag fluttered closer and closer. Black and white was all I saw.

I crossed the finish line and the flag dropped. I jammed both hands in the air and screamed, "I won. I actually won!"

I pulled into the pit and rocketed out of the go-kart. Mommy and Daddy were standing beside the track worker and owner.

"I won," I said. "Did you see me?"

"Awesome, Max!" Daddy said.

Mommy hugged and whispered in my ear. "I knew you could do it."

I felt a wet hand on my back. "Teamwork," Cody said, patting my shoulder. "That puddle will get you every time."

Just then Racer-X ran by, leaving a soggy trail on the sidewalk.

"We did it, Cody," I said. "We finally beat Racer-X."

Cody looked down; he was drenched from head to toe. "Well," he said. "I guess it's a small price to pay for a victory, but I didn't actually mean to hit that puddle. It just sort of happened."

We turned to Racer-X, who was talking to both the track worker and the owner. He pulled off his dripping jacket and hat. The dirty ball cap dropped to the ground and so did our jaws.

"What?!" I said.

Racer-X's long black hair tumbled onto her shoulders and stopped just above her waist. Then she turned and pointed at us.

"Holy-moly!" I screamed. "Racer-X is a girl!"

Cody just stared quietly. I nudged his mouth closed.

"Hey," I said. "Didn't you hear me? Look at that! She's been crushing us all day!"

Racer-X and the owner turned toward us.

"Uh-oh," I said softly. "Now we're in for it."

Cody just stood there like a statue.

"See, Daddy," Racer-X said. "I told you they could race." She looked us up and down. "As good as a boy can, anyways."

"Daddy?" I said, looking at the owner. "That's your daddy?"

She nodded and smiled.

"And one more thing," I said. "You're a girl!"

She squinted her eyes at me. "And?" she said.

"Is it so hard to believe that a girl has been beating the pants off you two all day?"

Cody finally snapped back and mumbled a few words. "Racer-X. Girl. Splash. Sorry."

"Racer-X?" she said. "Who's that? My name is Lucy."

"So," her daddy said, "these are the two you've been tangling with all day?"

She nodded.

He laughed. "By the looks of it, they got you at turn six."

"Sure did," she said.

"But you think they can handle it?" he asked.

"I'm telling you they can hang," Lucy said. "They cheated a bit with the puddle, but I guess that's racing." She squinted at Cody and his cheeks turned bright red.

"Sorry about that," he said softly.

Lucy smiled. "Sometimes you win and sometimes you just have fun."

Mommy and Daddy walked over.

"We're terribly sorry," Mommy said. She looked at us. "Ahem. Cody is there anything you'd like to say to this young lady?"

He looked up and swallowed. "I'm sorry for splashing you."

Lucy smiled.

"It's okay," she said. "I was already wet from the rain. No biggie."

Cody smiled and turned red again.

I jabbed him in the ribs. "What's wrong with you, weirdo?"

He coughed and stood up straight. "Nothing, Max. Be quiet."

The owner laughed and turned to Mommy and Daddy.

"Don't worry about it," he said. "From what Lucy tells me, these two are pretty skilled. She's basically grown up on this track."

"So that's how you got so good," I said.

"Yup," she said. "I spend whole weekends racing these tracks. I know every curve."

Lucy turned to her dad. "So, what do you say?" she said. "The park's almost empty anyways."

She tossed her long hair over her shoulder and tilted her head. "Pretty please? With sugar on top?"

Cody bumped me. "What's she doing?"

"I don't know," I said. "But I want to find out."

"Well, Lucy," he said. "I guess so. But only if their parents agree."

"Yay!" she said. Leaping up and down as she

clapped her hands. She turned to Mommy and Daddy. "Please?" she said, "Can they?"

"I'm sorry," Daddy said. "Have I missed something?"

"My dad is going to let us ride the super-fast go-karts!" she said. "The yellow ones."

I shook my head up and down so fast my neck hurt. Cody pressed his hands together and knelt in front of Mommy and Daddy. "I'll never ask for anything again as long as I live," he said. "Swear."

Daddy shrugged his shoulders. "Sounds okay to me," he said.

Mommy looked at Lucy. "And they did ruin your perfect record, didn't they?"

Lucy nodded her head. "It's payback time."

Mommy smiled. "I guess it's settled then," she said. "One more race."

"Whoo-hoo!" I said.

"Thanks," Cody said.

"This is going to be awesome," Lucy said. She high-fived her dad and looked at us. "Race you to the track!" She paused for a second and looked back. "Unless, of course, you're scared of getting beat by a girl."

We took off for the track and spilled into the first three go-karts.

The lights flickered from red to yellow to green and I stomped on the gas. Over the roaring engines and screeching tires I said softly to myself, "Now this is racing!"

From the Author

If you enjoyed this book, please leave an honest review. Word-of-mouth is truly powerful, and your words will make a huge difference. Thank you.

As you read this, I'm writing the next Max E. James adventure. For updates on new releases, promotions, and other great children's book recommendations, join my Kids' Club at:

http://www.maxejames.com/kids-club/

DON'T FORGET YOUR FREE DOWNLOAD

Type the link below into your browser to get started.

http://eepurl.com/cfcfkj

About the Author

J. Ryan Hersey is a devoted father and husband who lives in beautiful Hampton Roads, Virginia. His stories are inspired by the adventures he shares with his wife and two boys. He is author of the Max E. James children's series. To find out more or connect with him directly, visit his website at:

http://www.maxejames.com

About the Illustrator

Gustavo Mazali lives with his family in beautiful Buenos Aires, Argentina. Having drawn all his life, Gustavo has developed the unique ability to capture the essence of children in his art. You can view his portfolio at:

http://www.mazali.com

ABOUT THE EDITOR

Amy Betz founded Tiny Tales Editing after working as a children's book editor at several major publishing houses. She lives with her family in Bethel, Connecticut. You can learn more about Amy at:

http://www.tinytalesediting.com

ALL TITLES

Beach Bound
Birthday Bash: Part 1
Birthday Bash: Part 2
Fishing Fever
Winter Wipeout
Crash Course

Made in United States
North Haven, CT
26 May 2022